BLACK CHILD
and the
Discovery

Chris Perkins

Perkins, Chris BLACK CHILD / by Chris Perkins. Summary: A family
that once were black slaves, escaped and landed in the year of 2018

[1. Science Fiction- Fiction 2. Dark Fantasy – Fantasy]

Printed in the U.S.A. First American Edition, April 7th, 2018

We try to produce the most beautiful books possible, and we are
extremely concerned about the impact of our manufacturing process on
the forests of the world and the environment as a whole. Accordingly, we
made sure that all of the paper we used contains 30% post-consumer
recycled fiber. We love those who care and that is what we're all about!
CP Production Studios where dreams come true

DEDICATION

This book is dedicated to those who will remember

Abner for the rest of your days. Travel along with

him on his magical journey I also dedicate this book

to Isaac, and Chilita and to all of you that stuck with

Abner till the end!

Contents

ACKNOWLEDGMENTS

To my wonderful readers

grab some popcorn and when you read open

your imagination. HAHAHA, that's what I do!

INTRODUCTION

Many people might start out an "Intro to The Black Child" by probably giving you a summary of the first book, but not me. Nope. Once you have read The Black Child, you will realize what has truly changed and what can we change in America. Many of us will look at things differently. Not just things, but, people meaning race. I will give you a fact this book is not about race. This book I call the magical eye-opener has a big twist that none of you will expect!

You see, this book is told by the daughter of the parents, but it won't feel that way. Abraham the protector of the family is not just a regular, amazing person, but, a man who truly loves his family. Though in these times there was a forced separation that made their bond even stronger. The mother by the name of Elizabeth is a strong black woman who is also brave, but, fearful because of what happened to her and her loved ones.

The mystery and magic that happened inside of the black child caused them to get back what was once taken from them. You cannot fall in love with this family eagerly anticipating their next adventures, feeling their emotions, laughing along with jokes, and just feeling satisfied when you close the book. That is what a truly classical and historical book is, and the Black Child is truly classical and historical.

Abraham is this person who has this power that's given to him. There are some parts of the story that will cause you to bite your nails in suspense. Wondering what will happen to the family or will they be stuck in this forever. These characters seem like such real people that you almost feel their emotions. You can feel their anger, happiness, embarrassment, confusion, pride, and annoyance, their energy is so strong.

Over the past century's my people have been destroyed though I felt guilty because I couldn't stop it. As I watch the pain from my mother's eyes drop to the ground as she watches my father neck hanged bent from the tree. I scream to the sky give me a chance to live another life. So that I can see that there was a change in my future. I lived a day of nightmare and terror and the people who do such things laugh at the sight of pain and blood.

My people sang a song that was not for the voice of a human but to the people I knew that were once kings and queens. I say once again the day will come when we will get back what was ours.

A family I once knew flew away from me and now they are living the future I wish my family had the experience to see. –
Author Chris Perkins

BIRTH

It is now the year of 1926. The day I was born. Screaming, I hear as my mother is giving birth to my baby brother. Four men of the color white, came storming in trying to find out the commotion. They see a baby boy still connected to its mother womb.

A man by the name of Jeffery grabbed the knife and cut the umbilical cord. My father Abraham was not in the cabin at the time because he was still picking cotton in the fields. He had to work extra hard because his count was low last time. As punishment, our master whipped him with many stripes. Scars that no man can handle, engraved into my father's skin. Jeffery grabbed the baby boy, he raised it to his eye level and said,

"I know just where to put you! You're going to grow up strong and fast! As a cotton picking nigger"!

He chuckled to himself. My mother who my father calls Elizabeth, acted quickly trying to get hands on her baby boy. Jeffery quickly punches Elizabeth! She faints out cold! I scream for my mother,

"Mommy"

Jeffery looks at me and says,

"You outta learn from your mother, You niggers better stay in your lane!"

Tears drop from my face onto my mother's hand. Jeffery leaves, outside the cabin. Abraham stares from a distance hidden behind a bush. He sees Jeffery coming out of the cabin, carrying something in his hand. From a distance, Abraham could not see what it was. Including it was a dark and a silent night.

After no longer seeing Jeffery, Abraham runs into the cabin. The minute he storms in, he can feel the tension within the atmosphere. The floor and sheets were covered with blood. He can see the fear in Elizabeth's eyes.

"What Happened"! Said, Abraham

Elizabeth broke down crying. No words were needed, and he knew what had happened. Anger falls upon Abraham, emotion filled the room. It was so heavy I even felt it as a child. My father wanted to do something but, my mother stopped him from proceeding in action.

Abraham punches the wall, I was startled, I begin to cry because we all knew there was nothing we can do. My father stops suddenly, Silence was within the room. He then says,

"I'm getting our son back"

"But, how"! You know we can't do nothing!

says Elizabeth

Abraham yelled with all his might, with

tears dropping down to the surface of the

wooden floor. Snot and slobber covered

his face as he was filled with such raged.

"I don't care! Can we at least try"?

What are you planning to do?

Abraham gives Elizabeth no answer! He

stares at her and answers her within his

eyes. She became silent suddenly. Abraham opens the door behind him and slams it after he leaves out of it.

After leaving the cabin located near the women's and child side, where no negro male is allowed. He runs to find where Jeffery took his son. Abraham is discreet and silent. The thoughts that are running through his mind is beyond what any father shouldn't have to think!

Is my son dead? Are they going to kill my son? Abraham knows where his son is but, it will be very difficult crossing the field to get to the mansion.

A total of 12 white men with rifles covered the floor. Patrolling every corner and every hidden place within the field.

Abraham did not know how he would be able to do this. He has no weapons. Behind him, he hears a branch break. There were two white men behind him! He holds his breath and slows down his heart.

"Ricky, you hear something"?

"No! It could be a raccoon again!"

"mmhmm," says, Ricky

The bearded white riflemen. Gazed real hard at the bush, Abraham was hiding in! Saved by the voice of another white rifleman.

"You coming or what!"

Ricky looks at the white riflemen, and looks back at the bush!

"Yeah, I'm coming"!

Abraham starts breathing again. He gasped for air. Abraham choked and held his chest. He recovered quickly. Sneaks from outside the bushes and runs to the barn located near the cotton field. It was dark but, the only light by the barn was in front of it. Like a spotlight, waiting to catch something. By the barn, he can hear another two white men talking, having an enjoyable conversation nude models in the Playboy magazine.

Abraham has not heard of such thing, so he really didn't know what they were discussing. His focus was rescuing his son. Abraham hides once again. When the two white men pass from by the barn.

Abraham sneaks towards the mansion. Colorful and lighted well. It was guarded like the military base. A few yards from the mansion you can see another slave like myself being whooped. There was a total of 3 men that surrounded him.

It was as if they were playing a game and the slave was a toy. All the attention was on the slave being beaten to death. It was so terrifying, I felt like I was the one being beaten. Before, I move to my location Abraham sees Jeffery holding his son he was. It was nothing Abraham could do at the moment!

Jeffery was surrounded by **white riflemen**. From afar off, you can hear Jeffery shout,

"We got another nigger baby!"

White rifle men looked at it and said,

"Woah, that's an ugly motherfucker!"

Another **white rifleman** said,

"That nigger right there is going to be useful and I'm going to make sure of that!"

Everyone surrounded by Jeffery laughed, those who were white! Abraham witnessed the whole thing, his heart begins to boil with anger. Abraham knew that he needed a plan. He runs back to the men's cabin. When he opened the door, all the male negro slaves inside focused their eyes towards the wooden door!

They noticed the rage and anger on Abraham's face. Devon walks up to Abraham. Devon and Abraham were friends since they were stolen from their former master, who was hunt down and killed.

TROUBLE

I was at the age of 6. Abraham and Devon stood by each other.

Devon was also at the age of 6. Bounded in chains we were, Devon and Abraham transferred to a small town called **Drifton.** Drifton was a place no one has heard of. There were no other cars or carriages on the road. It was like as if we were being transferred like cattle. In a cage we were in, it smelled and reeked of bad odor.

Around us were empty fields. The fields were silent. The closer we got to the town, you can see heads starting to pop out from the fields. All were negro. I did not see one opposite color. Once arrived at the town, we noticed a gate it showed it's luxuriousness.

It was golden, like as if we were walking in an entrance of a castle to meet the king and queen.

We enter inside, from the outside it looks amazing, from the inside it's pretty but, ugly has taken over. Two **white riflemen** aimed their guns at Devon and Abraham after the carriage stopped! One **white rifleman** unlocked the gate.

"Come on nigger, get out of there!"

I proceeded with action and walked out of the cage. Devon, on the other hand, lets fear take over.

"Come on, now! Hurry Up!"

Still moving slow!

"You deaf nigga"

said, the **white riflemen** by the name of Andrew. Still, Devon did not move as quickly as Andrew wanted him to. Andrew took his rifle, turned it to the back and hit Devon's knees. Devon screamed with pain, tears fell from his face.

"Get up nigger, before I pull you out!"

Devon starts to move but, he can't contain himself. The **white riflemen** Andrew picked him up. He ripped off Devon's shirt and tied him to a tree. He grabbed a whip and prepared to beat Devon for his rebellion. Before, the whip released. The master came out and said, "and what the hell are you doing? "

Andrew replied.

"Teaching, this nigger how to be respectful!"

The master replied.

"You're not going to lay a finger on that boy! That's my money!"

Andrew replied.

"and why not?"

"You questioning boy?"

Said the master.

"No, sir!"

Said, Andrew. He un-tied Devon and Devon fell to his knees. The master walked up to him with a cloth and said,

"You know, I won't always be able to save you! You understand?"

Devon shook his head yes. Then the master said,

"Good!"

You're going to be working in the fields. Laughter comes from out of the master's belly.

"I'ma work you harder than no other nigger has worked before"

Out of the flashback we came out of. Devon walks up to Abraham.

"What's wrong? What they then do now?"

with eyes watered heavily. Abraham answered.

"They took my baby boy!"

The next day in the fields, all black negros were working hard with hmms and sweats. The sun felt as if it just gazing at us. Few fainted because of dehydration. The **white riflemen** rushed us to move faster but, our bodies were telling us differently.

As Abraham continues with his daily task. He then, sees a white woman dressed fancy. The reason she caught Abraham's attention because she was holding his baby boy. Abraham continues to stare, he was caught looking by one of the **white riflemen.**

"Hey, Nigger!"

Abraham doesn't turn around! The **white riflemen** approach him.

"I said, Hey, Nigger."

Abraham turns around and looks at the white riflemen out of fear.

"You hear me calling you Nigger"?

"No sir I didn't"

Abraham begins to stutter as the words come out of his mouth.

The white riflemen mock him.

"Ah N N N N No No Sir" He bust out of laughter. Oh, you a dumb nigger.

The white riflemen looks and sees the white woman dressed fancy walking into the house of the master.

"You have better not been looking at the master's daughter nigger"

"No sir I wasn't "

"Hmm," the white riflemen mumbles while looking at Abraham with his dead eye.

The white riflemen walk away and Abraham continues to work!

Inside the master's house, the white fancy woman enters.

Inside looked gorgeous full of royalty. It looks as if it was a historical museum. Walking around was negro maids who looked more healthy than the ones who were picking cotton outside. Their appearance was glooming and not one outfit had a scuff or hole in it. On the right of me, I can see the living room leading to the library and on the left, I see a dining area as elegant it can be. A giant statue was in the middle of the floor with two spiral stairs leading to the upward floor. One stair on the left and the other on the right. Pass the statue was the kitchen filled in it were the negro maids preparing dinner. As the white woman in fancy clothing walks inside she turns to the right towards the library. Inside was her mother the master's wife.

"Danielle," the mother says, with complete joy.

"Mother I haven't seen you in ages," She says while giving her mother a long-lasting hug.

"You never told me and your father you were coming back from Paris"

"Mother that's because I wanted it to be a surprise"

A black negro walks in and pours the master's wife tea as she does on a regular basis. As the negro maid pours tea for the Danielle, Danielle stops her.

"No that's fine let me do it myself. You've been working hard enough already!"

The mother is shocked and snaps.

"Danielle stop being foolish and let the nigger pour you some tea!"

"Mother, I said I can do it myself"

"I don't give a damn what you said I said let the nigger pour you the tea."

The negro maid puts down the bottle but, before she does the mother shouts.

"Put down that bottle and I'll hang you myself"

"Mother"

The master's wife walks up to the negro maid and to Danielle. She then, grabs the tea and pours it on the negro maid and slaps Danielle.

"Don't you ever disrespect me in front of a negro again"

She turns around to the negro maid and says

"Don't you have work to do"

The negro maid walks back to the kitchen drenched in tea.

Outside is Brandon, Danielle's brother see's a pretty negro in the field. He grabs her and tells her to

"Come on"

He pulls her, you can tell he is hurting her by her facial expression. Everyone in the field noticed what was going on.

Once inside the barn, Brandon told the negro slave to strip.

The woman shook her head no!

"I said Strip down"

The negro woman still did not want to strip down she shook her no yet again with tears going down her face as she covers herself.

Brandon walks over and smacks the negro woman. He then unbuckles his belt. The woman starts crying yelling stop! The negro's and the white riflemen hear it as clear as day. Some of the women in the field were shedding tears. Brandon rips her dress showing her fully nude body. He then begins to rape the negro woman grunting back in forth. The negro woman continues to scream. So, loud that it caught Danielle's and the master's wife attention. They storm outside not running but, walking at a fast pace. Danielle bursts into the barn and sees her brother raping the negro woman.

"Oh my god, What are you doing get off of her!"

Brandon launches off still bare naked covering himself

"Danielle, I didn't know you were back from Paris"

The master's wife walks in and that's when Brandon becomes afraid.

"Explain Yourself"

Brandon does not respond.

"No answer," the mother says

"I"

"You had your chance to speak now it is my turn" says the master's wife.

You are a disgrace to this family. You have cut yourself from this family the minute you put your dick into a negro woman. Out

of all the whites in this world, you decided

to take advantage of what your father

owns. Your father will be very

disappointed but, because he is not here

right now I am going to take matters into

my own hands because you are my child

apparently. Since you decided to fuck a

negro woman your penis is now poisoned

and you have cursed this family. In order

for us to keep this family pure we must

cleanse it's evil.

The mother walks over to the horse stable and sees a sharp knife. By the horse stable, there is a furnace. The master's wife lights the furnace and she heats the knife.

She then orders two white riflemen to hold down her son. Brandon starts to scream no!

"Apparently you don't know what that means neither do I"

She grabs her sons penis and cuts it off.

Danielle was unpleasant by what she saw so she vomited in the horses stable next to her.

Brandon starts screaming. The master walks inside!

"What the hell is going on!"

"Ask your son!"

The master sees the negro woman fully naked and understands what had happened!

"Take him inside!"

THE ESCAPE

Rewinding back to when the commotion first started happening. Abraham is in the field continuing to pick cotton. The white riflemen leave the area to attend the chaos going on inside the horse barn.

When there were no white riflemen insight Abraham runs towards the white house.

No one noticed but the negro slaves in the field. He sneaks inside after the mother and Danielle leaves the house.

Inside he searches for his baby boy! Around the corner he sees a negro maid holding it and feeding it. The negro maid was startled when she saw Abraham. Abraham puts his index finger to her lips and says

"Shhh"

Abraham grabs the baby and food for the baby. He sneaks back out of the house and heads towards the women and children area. Inside he sees Elizabeth and his daughter. At first, Elizabeth thought it was Jeffery but, after she saw that it was Abraham she lit up with joy.

"Daddy," The daughter says

Elizabeth runs and hugs Abraham and kisses him a million times.

"We have to go!"

"Abraham where we gonna go there are white men everywhere"

"I don't know we just going keep on running"

"Hurry up let's go"

Abraham looks out the door to see if anyone is around! After he sees that it is clear they run into the forest next to the women and children's area. Elizabeth and Abraham run their fastest they see that their daughter is lagging behind so Abraham gives Elizabeth the baby and picks the daughter up. They continue running.

As the darken, the sky fell upon them! Energy has not left Elizabeth and Abraham. Back on the plantation, the mother notices that it was to quiet in the house. Outside it's time to do a count of the collected cotton. The white riflemen notice that Abraham is not around!

"Something doesn't seem right! Ricky go see if you see that nigger Abraham if you do please drag that nigger to me"!

Ricky goes to the men section and opens the door. Everyone is startled. Where's Abraham! Everybody in the room looked at each other!

"Shit" Ricky says

He then runs to the bunker to see if his wife and daughter were there and there was no sight of any of them.

Ricky runs out screaming ring the alarm, ring the alarm we got us a runner.

The alarm goes off.

The white riflemen grab their guns from the gun rack and head towards the forest.

Inside the house a white riflemen storms

into the master's office and says

"Sir we got a problem!"

"Well don't spill it out all at once"

"That nigger Abraham escaped with his

wife, daughter, and son"

"How the hell did that happen?"

The master grabs his jacket and gun and gets on his horse.

Outside its about fifteen horse's and on foot was about six men with rifles.

"Let's go" the master shouts

Hearing the sound of the horses galloping.

From a distance, Elizabeth and Abraham hear the horses. They continue to run as fast as they can.

The white riflemen have torches in there hand speeding through the forest like a bolt of lightning. A white rifleman spots Abraham!

The white riflemen say

 "There that nigger goes over their" Abraham and Elizabeth keep running and spots a cabin close by.

Abraham shouts. "run to the cabin" Closer and closer the cabin gets and closer and closer the white riflemen gets to Abraham and Elizabeth. They finally reach the cabin. The front door is locked but, a haystack near them reaches the upper window.

Abraham quickly climbs it to see if the window is unlocked and it was.

He then jumps off the haystack and makes Elizabeth go first. He then puts the baby back into her arms and grabs the daughter.

Finally, Abraham climbs through the window and locks it. He covers it up with everything in sight. After that, he runs downstairs to block off the door. Which he did.

The white riflemen reach the cabin. They get off their horses and try to enter into the cabin. They can't enter in!

"Open this door Nigger Now" the master shouts

"On the count of three if you don't come out here! I swear I'm a burn this bitch to the ground. Now you don't want me to do that do you?" In a sweet kinda care but don't care voice.

Still no answer!

"You niggers really don't listen"

"Boys burn it down," the master says

The white riflemen throw their torches through the windows. Everything started to burn so quickly. You can hear their daughter screaming. The master started laughing. A few moments later they were surrounded by fire. Behind them was a closet. They enter inside covering the children's mouth. They continue to back up. The fire begins to burn the door. They back up even more.

Everything turns to black. All of a sudden you could not hear the fire nor smell it.

BLACK CHILD AND THE DISCOVERY

TIME WE FLEW

The family is in a crouched positioned in the corner of the closet. They lift their heads. Abraham sneaks to the door and the door handle is cold. He turns the knob.

When he opens the door there is no sign of ash nor is anything burnt. Everything is covered in cobbed web. As if the house was deserted for a long period of time.

Abraham walks around the house so as Elizabeth and the rest follows. They see a window and outside the window they see cars not horses and people walking with fashionable clothing. Not dressed like them of course! They were shocked! They didn't know what had happened. Abraham opened the door and peeped through it and Elizabeth was underneath Abraham. They saw a black man with a white woman holding hands, they saw a black man in a business suit interacting with a white man laughing.

"Abe," Elizabeth said.

"Yeah"

"Is that a negro laughing with a white man"

"I think so"

Across the street they see a black man kissing a white girl.

"Oh that man is dead," Elizabeth says

The white man walked right past them without saying a word.

"Elizabeth" Abe says

"Yeah"

"Did that white man pass that negro and white girl kissing each other?"

"I think so"

They hear a train but, didn't know where it was coming from.

They scream because they thought they were going to get hit by it. The people on the sidewalk near them looked at them and they shut the door.

"Abraham there gonna kill us"

They barricade the door and a few moments later noticed that no one was coming. They unbarricaded the door and noticed that people were wearing happy new year signs that said 2018. A guy approaches the door and they close the door yet again.

He knocks on the door! No answer

"Nerdy white guy- Hey I saw you answer the door it's new years eve"

No answer again they hide by the window. So the nerdy white guy looks through the window.

(Nerdy guy laughing) Caught Ya! Laughing out loud!

Everyone screams.

" Open the door I'm not gonna hurt ya. You guys are acting like someone is trying to kill you"! Laughing out loud

Abraham and Elizabeth looked at each other and opened the door.

Ah! That's funny I never met black Amish people before! Never mind that happy new year. I'm Frank and welcome to 2018.

"Wait did you say 2018," Abe asked

"Yeah, Oh I forgot you don't have TVs"

Anyways come to this party we are having downtown in times square.

"Where," Elizabeth asked

"New York times Square Duh! I don't think ill be able to make it as an Amish it's too difficult"

See you there yeah okay.

The nerdy guy leaves and Abraham closes the door. Feeling lost and confused they were. They began to question the word Amish the nerdy male compared them to.

Elizabeth turns to Abraham and says "what is Amish"? Abraham responds with the same equal confusion.

"I don't know".

Trying to put everything together stuck in another dimension and inside a home filled with dust and white sheets. They continue to search the home of the unknown. Upstairs was a library and inside this library was a black book heavy filled with many pages larger than a dictionary! It caught the attention of Abraham and Elizabeth because a light source lit the darkness from it. It glowed in the eye of a human. Abraham approached the book and reached to fill the surface of this unknown discovery!

A sudden impact came upon Abraham – a large energy ring went through the abandoned house and touched everyone that was in it. There was no sudden change afterward everything felt the same.

Abraham opens the book – Inside the book was an empty page for page. The book was completely blank. Shocked Abraham was – when he closes the book a title appears on the cover named the Black Child. Abraham rubs the stitching of the words, raised print and the color of gold.

A loud sound of glass breaking hits the eardrum of Elizabeths and Abrahams ear. Immediately the light turns to black. Abraham and Elizabeth run downstairs. They see the shattered glass but, caused by

I the daughter of Abraham and Elizabeth. Instead of my mother being upset she comforts me out of fear. The tightness of the hug I was given felt as if she was physically transferring her love spiritually.

I remember after my mother released from me she gazed into the glass that was shattered on the ground. a flashback of them being in the fire appeared in it. Abraham saw the same thing. Beside him was a mirror and in that mirror appeared a live image of his master on the horse running towards him. It was all in the imagination. Abraham out of fear shattered the glass, I screamed with a strong reaction hiding in my mother's chest.

Stay away from the mirrors Abraham. Elizabeth stands up and says

"well this place isn't going to clean itself"

She walks over and grabs the broom and starts cleaning. In the closet near the back door were cleaning products with gloves. She handed me a cleaning product called mr.clean. Appeared on it was a white man with a shiny head and a scrubbing brush. After reading the label on the back of the second product Elizabeth picked out which was in written red print said,

"Keep Out Of The Reach Of Children"

My mother quickly snatches it out of my hands.

"Thank you," said Elizabeth talking to the cleaning products as if they were human beings.

She closes the door to the closet and begins cleaning. She removed the white sheets that were covering the furniture. Abraham helped her clean as well. Everything was in the middle of the floor and had to be pushed back into the position it used to be in. The only reason they knew where the furniture was supposed to go was because on the ground were shapes made out of dust fitting each object that was located in each room.

It was as if we were putting pieces together on a puzzle and already knew how it was supposed to go. After they finished, the place was spit clean. It had a nice wood smell – the outdoor feeling.

Elizabeth knew not what to do they have never lived together before this is the very first time they were ever connected as a family. Downstairs was a bedroom and inside was a bed. Abraham lays me on the bed and my mother and father both kissed me on the forehead. Next, to me, they lay my baby brother. They keep the door open with a nightlight found inside the room. When my mother switched it on it played a sweet melody and circling around was a girl in a pink dress dancing.

Elizabeth and Abraham exit the room and head upstairs to another bedroom located near the discovered library.

BLACK CHILD AND THE DISCOVERY

DISCOVERY

Inside the room, Abraham takes off his shirt. When he takes off his shirt Elizabeth notices that there are no scars on his back.

"Abe"

"Whats wrong Elizabeth"

"Yo scars are gone"

Abraham was trying to feel his back and the spots he knew had deep scar tissue damage he felt and none there was. He then tries to find a mirror and forgot that he destroyed them all.

Tears fell from his face. His wife comforted him embraced he felt. He turned to her, nose and lips rubs against the side of her rich milk chocolate skin. Their lips meet, satisfaction she feels, a strong force of energy comes upon Abraham.

He rips the clothing off of her. Underneath she had nothing. A beautiful bush she had and her nipples looking pure. Her eyes met Abrahams eyes meeting each other spiritually and physically. Abraham picks up Elizabeth and lays her on the bed. Kissing her neck then her breast then down to her belly. She quickly turns around and shouts

"Please" a soft but, seductive moan

Abraham starts to make love to his wife moving in back and forward motion. He started off slow but, then he begins to pick up speed. Her moan sounded like no other. She pleased by every touch.

She turns around and starts to take control by flipping Abraham to his back. She rides Abraham hard and fasts. Her eyes rolled back to the back of her head. She begins to bite his lip. Moaning louder and louder.

Seductive sighs she makes.

"Yes, Yes, Yes" Elizabeth moaning

Their skin became moisten. Sweat dripping onto the bed. Bed begins to squeak.

Hearing Abraham about to cum!

"Ohhhhh"

A short pause of breathing occurred

Then he releases a long breath into thin air.

Elizabeth lay next to him and said.

Is this a sign from God?

What Abraham responded

Are we given a chance to live life freely as a negro family! God always has his ways of doing things said Abraham. On the end table near the bed on Abrahams left side was the flyer given to him by the white nerdy guy that visited earlier. Abraham picks up the flyer then looks at Elizabeth.

Let's go have fun there's still a new world we must explore. Clothes they had none so they went how they were to times square. It was a dark and cold night. Barefooted they both were walking the streets of New York. Abraham wraps his arms around her to give her warmth. They did not know where they were going. Another light source appeared guiding them to somewhere of course they followed. A long line full of light in the form of smoke went through the alley and paused until we followed.

It led us through the streets of New York finally we arrive! Abraham and Elizabeth were amazed at what they saw.

"Oh my Abe look at what then happen over the past decades"

They saw people with drinks in their hands smiling and laughing. They even saw this crazy man. Screaming

"You have been Warned Fuck the Government"

Abraham approaches the crazy man and says.

"Who is this government that was fuck"

The crazy man burst out a loud and obnoxious laughter causing Abraham and Elizabeth to flinch from it.

"Oh you don't know"

The government is after you! Aliens are among us we must protect ourselves.

Abraham asked and how must we protect ourselves from this government and alien you speak of.

Elizabeth whispers to Abraham and says.

"We have to get back they are here"

The crazy man responds to Abrahams question.

"Listen very closely".

the crazy man says

"Grab the aluminum foil and wrap it around your whole body just like I did see"

Abraham replies

"Are you sure this is going to protect us"

"I'm positive"

With the ugliest grin on his face smiling like never before in a creepy sort of way.

Abraham wraps the foil around Elizabeth and Elizabeth wraps the foil around Abraham. When they finished wrapping themselves the man who was out of it vanished.

Elizabeth said to Abraham – We are given so many signs we have to get back to the kids.

They did not know how to get back to the house because the light source never appeared again. So here they are lost in the city of New York.

They found times square. They walked through it and noticed how much different races were all together for they only knew of only one race everything else was a blur.

An Asian walked past Elizabeth smiling screaming happy new year's. As they continue to walk they hear a man screaming Hot dogs get your hot dogs here.

"Food," said Elizabeth

they approach the hot dog stand to try to

reach for the hotdog the man hit there

hand

"Hey Hey Hey you got to pay for those!

"So what do you want on them"

What do we want? said, Abraham

"Yeah, I got relish. Onion grilled or raw, pickles mustard ketchup and hot buns and oh yeah hotdogs"

"We will take everything" said Elizabeth

"Okay two hotdogs with everything coming up

That will be 6 dollars do you want anything to drink with that. I got a grape soda, Fanta orange, Hawaiian punch, sprite or Coca Cola"

They both choose the coke product

"Okay, your total is now 8 bucks". Abraham and Elizabeth looked around because they didn't know what he meant when he said bucks or dollars.

"Come on look in your pocket and give me the eight bucks". Abraham reached into his pocket and he found money but, it wasn't 8 dollars it was 444 dollars.

"Woah I only asked for 8 bucks give me that 20 and ill give you change" said the hot dog man.

He gave me back 12 dollars Abraham looked at Elizabeth.

"Is this what money looks like".

As they eat their food they both fall in love with it. It is there first time ever trying a hot dog.

The nerdy white guy sees them but before he does he was walking down the street blowing the happy new year whistle.

"Hey, you made it and you brought awesome outfits to wait! Let me guess your tin man from wizard of Oz!"

"The tin man" Abraham asked.

"Yeah from the movie wizard of oz you never saw it".

"Whats a movie" they both asked.

"Are you serious"! He starts laughing while snorting clapping his knees "Oh your serious you two are not from New York are you"!

Fear they both felt when the question was asked! "Never mind that come on we are missing the party"! he grabs Abraham and Elizabeth.

It was this place called The Time the sign was made out of neon and in the front of the door was a big mist of fog. People stood there smoking and talking amongst each other. They had on outfits as well, so Abraham and Elizabeth blended in with them.

Inside was amazing there played loud music. Abraham and Elizabeth covered their ears. Surrounded by them were people dancing barely hard to move through the crowd. They saw black men dancing with white women and white men

dancing with a black woman.

I don't think I caught your names said the

nerdy white guy.

Abraham and Elizabeth responded and

said their names

"Abraham" said Abraham

"Elizabeth" said Elizabeth

Frank offered them drinks. Let me get 3 shots of Tequila. They never tasted alcohol, so they really didn't know what they were up to. Frank started dancing as he picks up the drinks to hand to Abraham and Elizabeth.

Try this he says

Frank throws it down his throat making a grunting noise afterward because of the stinging and burning feeling he felt from the liquor.

Abraham and Elizabeth did the same and oh boy was there a different reaction. They both acted if they were going to die. Holding their necks,

"he's trying to kill us" they both said.

Frank started laughing

"No" he said

"I'm not trying to kill you that's what you're supposed to feel after drinking liquor after all it wasn't that bad you two are rookies".

Abraham and Elizabeth get up off the floor slowly. Frank asked did they want another one they both shook there heads NO!

He then shouted!

"Let's dance"! He then, walks into the crowd and starts dancing left foot to the right foot. Abraham and Elizabeth just looked at each other.

Once they made eye contacted they hunched their shoulders and walked into the crowd with Frank. The song kept saying "lets party" in a female voice, the beat was a fast tempo. Turns out the party that they were at or the so-called club The Time was a rave party. The tempo of the beat got faster and faster! Frank was dancing hard. Abraham and Elizabeth were confused and were a bit off beat.

"Woo" Frank shouted! "Are you guys having fun"?

Abraham and Elizabeth give him the thumbs up when Frank turns around and continues dancing they both make their way to the exit

.

Outside they now are still cold and dark. Worried about their children so they continue to find there way home.

Appears yet again out of the blew the light trail. Abraham and Elizabeth follow the trail but it doesn't lead them to the home. It leads them to a bookstore. For some strange reason, it was still open and all the rest of the stores were closed because of the holiday.

They both walk inside. It was an old bookshop no one was in the front area. They search the store and the back near the corner was a shelf and on that listed the black child same book as the one from the home black book size of the dictionary with gold lettering. I and Elizabeth were amazed as we had seen this book before. Written inside the book scary to Elizabeth and Abraham. Everything they did from the beginning of the discovery of the closet that flew them into the future was written inside of it. Including them finding the bookstore. The words begin to write themselves Abraham noticed it. It was spelling out,

"Abraham stood looking at the book, behind him was a man who was dressed in his sleep apparel wearing pajamas and a matching hat." After reading that last part, Abraham turns around and there was a man dressed in sleep Apparel he had on Pajamas with a matching hat.

He shouted, "Can I Help You"?
Abraham and Elizabeth both startled and confused.

The man responded and said, "What are you looking at over there"?

He saw that they were looking at the black book and got really angry.

"How did you find this"?

He saw that the book was opened, and he read what it had said.

This cant be he said, this was just a myth are you truly Abraham and Elizabeth.

Abraham responded and said yes.

 The man began to leap with joy and said "for my name isn't *Gurtle* the legends have finally come true".

"What legends"? Abraham asked!

The old man continues to leap for joy ignoring the fact that Abraham is asking him a question.

Abraham repeats the question once more.

"What Legend"?

The old man stops leaping and freezes no longer than two seconds.

"You want to know about the legends"

"Yes Please," said Elizabeth

she was very curious about what was being said about her and her husband.

"Follow me"

Elizabeth and Abraham follow *Gurtle*.
Gurtle turns off the lights and puts up the closing sign. Looking out the window as if he was not trying to be seen. He leads us into the backroom. Back there was a stairway that led to the lower level. Below was a room filled with scrolls and artifacts. He turned on the light, it lit half of the room some of the corners were still covered with a black shadow.

Gurtle went to the bookshelf located on the right side of us. On that bookshelf was a book called the Black Koning and Koningin meaning the *black King and Queen* but Abraham and Elizabeth do not know such thing. *Gurtle* opens the book to read the prophesy written back in 1358 B.C

Long ago in a village filled with gold and riches. A world where everyone knew everyone and a place where people were strong and brave. That place was not there for long. A horrible darkness was ahead.

A dark shadow controlled by Balsak came and attacked the village. Appeared in the sky was a great sphere sent down by the creator. Inside the sphere was a child. No one could see this child for it looked as if a sphere was the womb and it was still inside of its sack.

It saved the village from the attack of Balsak so the king and his people began to worship there savor. Came down another, when the second arrived the spheres began to open. Crying was a baby boy and in the second sphere was a baby girl.

Years have passed and grown these two were. The girl was named after the queen Raiden and the boy was name Abner meaning the *God of light.*

The book says that Balsak returned.

Elizabeth stopped *Gurtle* from continuing

"What does this have to do with me and Abraham"

Gurtle responds.

"Why are you so impatient! Fine I'll just skip ahead"?

"No you don't have to do that please continue," said Abraham

"Very well then" *Gurtle* replied.

"Where was I oh yes"

Balsak attacked the village once again. Abner and Radian stood to fight yet again Balsak was defeated but, this time he put a spell on the land and village.

The village was cursed for years. The home of the brave was destroyed. Abner said to his people that one day he will rain once more before his death. Century's people have waited.

A bird gave a sign to the people that Abner has returned. Many say it was sent from the gods above.

The sign contained details of a child birthing from a mother name Elizabeth and father name Abraham.

"Your newborn baby is Abner"

Elizabeth and Abraham were left in shock because how did *Gurtle* know that Elizabeth had a newborn baby boy.

"How do you think you got here"? said *Gurtle.*

Those were the gifts of Abner one of them was "Teleportation".

Throughout your journey, you will discover more gifts and abilities within your son. There is a total of 12 gifts you will discover those I cannot name for it is forbidden to speak of before it is written in the book. Follow the golden trail and it will lead the way.

Gurtle quickly closes the book and says well that was a remarkable story huh! Laughing out loud! Alright, out you must go there are many adventures ahead of you. I wish you the best of luck and I promise you this! It's not the last you will see me again. *Gurtle* says.

THE REVEAL

The golden trail appeared once more. The home they are now in, the kids were still asleep. Abraham and Elizabeth look inside of the room where I was sleeping. Abraham and Elizabeth stood they're looking at their son. For the things that were shown to them remained inside their head but, Abraham and Elizabeth became

more and more curious about the things
that were being said. They both went
upstairs to rest. As they rest Elizabeth
begins to dream. A nightmare was the
dream she had – causing her to shiver and
twitch. Heavily drenched in sweat. Two
horses one was brown and the other was
white. By looking at the horse you would
think that there was a man riding on it
with a torch in his hand. This was
complete opposite there were horses, no
man but, a lit torch. Her husband and
children were in ghost form and all that

was left was her still in human form. She screamed waking her up in the reality. By the time she woke up, it was 8:30 am in the morning. Laying next to her was no one. Abraham was found downstairs yet staring at his son.

"I would have thought you be in bed a little longer from all the hell we been through" said Elizabeth.

She noticed Abraham staring at their son and said.

"You don't really believe that's true, do you"?

Abraham turned to her and replied

"You saw it for yourself that book said our names – I thank god since I landed here but, this still does not make any sense to me".

I wake up out of bed – there stood my mom and dad. Happy my mom was – I walk up to her and lay my head to her stomach. She embraces me with her love by rubbing my hair with her hand all the way to my upper back.

She then asks,

"Are you hungry sweetie"?

I respond with a nod and into the kitchen, my mother went. I never saw my mother cook a meal but, I do know that she cooked in the white house before she got kicked out for being pregnant.

While Elizabeth cooks in the kitchen, Abraham discovers a television that is covered in dust and completely turned off. Abraham does not know what this is but he is curious anyways for they did not have televisions back then. He plugs it into the wall and pops up a picture. The first channel shows cartoons and Abraham is completely amazed at what he is seeing. He calls Elizabeth in and she is in awe.

Abraham then changes the channel. The second channel shows the planet of the apes.

"Elizabeth they got monkeys on this thing here" said Abraham with a big grin on his face.

Elizabeth says "Oh just beautiful I never saw what a monkey look like before".

Me either while laughing with his hands still on the screen.

The next channel appears the Playboy network. Breast filled the screen of black and white women. Vaginas and butts were shown on the television as well.

Abrahams and Elizabeth face turned from a smile to a frown.

Abraham quickly unplugs the television.

"Were they showing private parts on that box there"? Said Elizabeth

"Mhmm"! Abraham

And were those white woman too!

"Mhmm"! Abraham said again

"This world then change big and big I see"

"Mhmm"! Abraham says yet again while Elizabeth walks back into the kitchen.

Abraham tries to turn back on the television and Elizabeth shouts

"Don't touch that box anymore"!

After she said that a knock on the door there was. Spooked Abraham was because no one knew that they stayed at this address. Abraham looks out the window and sees no one by the door. He opens the door to find a brown letter laying flat on the welcome mat. Covering the letter was a red ribbon and a red fancy stamp from a drop of candle wax.

Abraham picks up the letter and turns it around. The front showed wording that spelled out THE REVEAL. He closes the door and shows the letter to Elizabeth.

"Well open it she says"

Abraham opens the letter but, inside was an owl feather. Abraham and Elizabeth were both confused about what they received. The owl symbolizes wisdom and higher power sent from the sky gods but, Abraham and Elizabeth did not know that.

In Abraham's hand still holds the owl feather.

Within minutes it vanishes leaving a mist behind. Scared they both were – they did not understand how this object vanished before their eyes.

Their son still asleep inside the room woke up instantly, crying they heard. Everyone in the room went into the bedroom where he was located. Elizabeth picks him up embracing him with love.

She brings him into the kitchen because she thinks he is hungry. Hungry he was but, that is not the reason he was crying.

While feeding her son she notices a scar on his left forearm. The scar was a full circle. Three different layers they were in. The first inner circle contained the feather and everything else was blank. It looked almost like a tattoo.

Elizabeth became worried trying to rub the tattoo off of the baby but, it just would not remove.

Elizabeth called Abraham into the kitchen.

"Abe", she shouts

"What is it Elizabeth"? as he storms into the room

"Look"!

"How did this happen"?

"It was the letter"!

"What are you talking about"?

"Look again but, closely"

Abraham looks at his son's arm and there he saw the feather. Quickly Abraham falls to the ground backing up till his back hits the wall. Anything that was in his way fell over.

Abraham begins to have a mental breakdown episode.

"No! No! No! this can't be true"! says, Abraham.

Hands on his head Elizabeth asks a question

"Gurtle was telling the truth all along. Our son saved our lives".

WHO AM I

7 years have passed the boy we all know as the one who bears the gifts is now at the age of 7 years old. Though time has flown no one has aged but, their son and time remained in the year of 2018. Things began to feel strange to Elizabeth and Abraham. Though they were living better

lives something still felt off. They knew that their job was to protect their son. Abraham and Elizabeth still have questions, but all is not revealed in the book of guidance.

Alone on his bed lays the son of Abraham and Elizabeth. The bedroom was dark no light to be seen. The light was trying to leak in but could not because of the shades that blocked its entry.

In the room is a closet door made out of fine wood painted white. The doors crept

CHRIS PERKINS

open. Spooked he was! The son of Abraham and Elizabeth saw the eyes of a creature. It appeared to be a creature with wings. The creature slammed open the doors running and hiding behind the dresser. Near the son of Abraham and Elizabeth was a coin laying on top of the end table. He threw the coin and out ran the creature. The creature ran underneath his bed.

146

The son of Abraham and Elizabeth eyes widen for he was afraid of what it might be. He slowly looks underneath his bed and popping towards him is a baby dragon. It was the most beautiful dragon you can imagine. The wings of the dragon were rich with tiny crystals engraved into the skin. The son of Abraham and Elizabeth screamed startling the dragon. He can hear his parents coming downstairs. He covers the dragon with the blanket and flying open comes the door.

Abraham says

"What's going on? Are you okay"?

The son of Abraham and Elizabeth responded.

"Yeah, I'm fine dad I just fell out of bed".

"I'll get your mother" said, Abraham

"No"! screamed the son of Abraham and Elizabeth.

"It's okay, see I'm fine"! as he shows the father that he has no bruises or scratches.

Be careful says Abraham then closes the door afterward.

The son of Abraham and Elizabeth removed the cover from over the dragon.

Frightened the dragon was – a leak of light peaked through the shades. Still afraid the dragon hid in the shadow. The son of Abraham and Elizabeth started talking to the dragon to make it feel more comfortable.

Don't hide I'm not going to hurt you said the son of Abraham and Elizabeth. There was still

no response from the dragon for he was no longer afraid but shy. A few moments later out came the dragon walking slowly towards the son of Abraham and Elizabeth.

The son of Abraham and Elizabeth reached out his hand to touch the head of the dragon. The minute he touched the dragon – a vision appeared to him showing the life and birthing of the dragon. In the vision shown was of a boy with long white hair, he was sent to protect the son of Abraham and Elizabeth. The boy who had long white hair has the gift of a dragon. Which means that this boy can transform into a dragon anytime he wants to.

The dragon spoke to the son of Abraham and Elizabeth. He got spooked instantly. The boy with the long white hair cannot change into human form while in the 3rd dimension.

"What is your name" said the son of Abraham and Elizabeth?

"Prince Norm" said the dragon

"You're a prince" said the son of Abraham and Elizabeth.

"Yes and I am your servant your majesty" said *Price Norm.*

"Your majesty"? said the son of Abraham

"Do you not know who you are"? Said Prince Norm

The son of Abraham and Elizabeth shook his head no!

"You are Abner the god of light and ruler of many".

"My name is Abner" said, Abner

"For it is written about you in the book of legends have you not yet heard of such thing". Said Prince Norm.

Again, Abner shakes his head "NO"!

Prince Norm was amazed at what he was hearing.

"This is so amazing, I'm the first to meet the god of light and they sent me to protect you"! said Prince Norm.

"I was told to give you this by the gods" said Prince Norm

Prince Norm breathes in and exhales onto Abner giving him yet another gift. Appeared on his on his arm above the first circle and above the feather was an "eye of a tiger".

"Oh!, that's nice" said Prince Norm "the eye of a tiger is an amazing gift to have for it is very rare to have. The eye of the tiger makes you undefeatable".

"You may notice a sudden change in your eyes for you will now be able to see very well in darkness".

"Why do I need a protector"? says, Abner?

"For there is darkness in this world and many are aimed to harm and take the gifts away from you. For you are still a child as am I"! said Prince Norm.

"We must go your father is in trouble"! said Prince Norm.

"My father"? said Abner

Inside the library was Abraham returning back to the black book again. He tries to open the book but the book would not open.

Abraham made mistake by trying to force his way into the black book.

The room filled with darkness. No light there was and a red beautiful glow surrounded the book. Out the book came out a hand reaching towards Abraham. He immediately fell to the ground trying to escape.

Everyone in the house heard Abraham scream. Elizabeth comes running upstairs calling out Abrahams name.

"Abe" said Elizabeth

Trying to open the door leading to the library but it remained shut as if someone was holding the door on the other side. Abner and Prince Norm follow the mother upstairs. Prince Norm blows on the door luckily the mother did not see.

(לִפְתוֹחַ meaning OPEN!)

The door immediately opens. Laying on the ground they see Abraham and the hand still reaching out to Abraham.

Prince Norm stands in front of Abner.

לך מכאן שאני הנסיך נורם המגן של אבנר meaning ("Go away for I am Prince Norm the protector of Abner") !

The thing that was trying to attack Abraham disappeared. Abraham wakes up after passing out he sees a dragon next to Abner.

Abraham screams!

SURPRISE

Continuing from when Abraham screamed. Elizabeth got startled as well but, Abner and Prince Norm stood they're looking at the reactions from his mother and father.

"Son get away from that thing and get over here" says, Abraham.

Abraham started freaking out as if he was having a panic attack.

"I'm not going to hurt Abner"!

"What did you just call him"? Said Abraham.

"Abner the god of light"!

"How did you know that"? Said, Abraham

"For I am the protector sent to serve and look out for your son".

"Wait what are you"?

Abraham did not know what Prince Norm was because he has never seen such a creature. The only animal Abraham and Elizabeth saw were birds from when they chirp in the morning, Horses that were kept at the plantation and dogs. Though Abraham and Elizabeth have never seen good in a dog.

"Who are you? and What is your name"?

"So many questions you ask"! says Prince Norm. "For my name is Prince Norm and I have the gift of a dragon, therefore, that is what you're seeing".

I have a question? Said Prince Norm

"Have you not read the book for it is written of who I am".

I tried said Abraham but, the minute I tried to open it something bad happen.

"The book can only be opened once by hand once you have gotten the basic understanding of it then it seals itself. The only one who can open it is the one who bears the magic".

"That's nice to know"! said Abraham

"You all have so much to learn"! said Prince Norm. "For Abraham, you are a warrior and also the protector of Abner". "Elizabeth you birthed Abner from out of your womb so that is what is in him lies within you. You may have felt drained at times because you are in lack of your gift. Each of you has gifts that are used to protect Abner".

"Come"! says Prince Norm. centered in a circle surrounded by the support of Abner.

They gather around – before Prince Norm gives out the gifts he sees the daughter of Abraham and Elizabeth standing in the doorway.

Prince Norm saw her with his eyes closed. He opens his eyes quickly looking directly at the daughter of Abraham and Elizabeth.

"Ah – and who might this one be"?

"For her heart is filled with rage as do you, Abraham".

"For the both of our warriors did Prince Norm. Prince Norm. Inhales and exhales onto Elizabeth and gives her the gift of love. Elizabeth didn't have love because it was taken away from her at the plantation. She was also given appeared out of nowhere a necklace around her neck. silver it was. very precious it was. Prince Norm told Elizabeth that, that necklace will always remind her of Abner. Prince Norm turns to Abraham and says,

"yes I know you are a warrior. and yes we know that you are a protector of Abner. that is why you have the heart of a bull. Anything that comes between you and

your family and your loved ones. you will
always be rageful into protecting

them always. Though when Abner grows
up into a man he will not need much
protection. For by then he will be mature.
yes, I have been sent by the gods said
Prince Norm. but, we all have an agenda
here. We all have a job to do for this is the
season of training for Abner. you are not to
be responsible for anything that happens
to you while, you are at this age but, when
you're grown to a man. You will begin to
see and feel the results of all your actions.

That was said to me very clear by the gods and they wanted me to tell you that.

As a family you are strong. because of the unity. we must not let anyone come in between us. Abner for that is our main focus that is why you are truly here in this dimension for when you have completed this task you will be leveled up into another world.

"What do mean by another world"?

"Are you saying that we will no longer be apart of this earth"? Asked Abraham

"You still will be on this earth but in a different time frame. You would never go back in time you will always move forward".

"I must go for I am in need"said Prince Norm.

The prince (Dragon) vanishes into thin air. Afterward, Abraham gets up and storms out of the house because everything is too overwhelming for him. Alone he was and worried the others were. He walked down the sidewalk and saw a bar across the street.

Abraham does not know what a bar is nor does he know what they do inside of it. The only reason Abraham went inside because he saw that there were a lot of people coming in and out from it. It caught Abraham's attention.

Inside the bar no one noticed him but the bartender. For there were many races inside the bar. Whites, blacks, Asian,

Mexicans you name it. Abraham was shocked because a white woman who was the bartender spoke to him. The bartender asked Abraham.

"What can I get you, hun"?
Abraham stood they're looking around – he did not know that she was talking to him although he was the only one she was looking at.

She asked again.

"Are you just gonna stand their or your gonna get something to drink"?

Abraham moves forward and sits down on the stool.

"What do you have" said, Abraham

The bartender chuckled and said liquor.

Abraham said

"okay I'll have that"!

She laughed again then said which one.

"Surprise me" Abraham says to the bartender.

"What's your name"? she asked him

"Abraham and yours"

"Belle", she says to Abraham

"You're not from here are you, Abraham"?

When she asked that Abraham got startled
because he thought she knew. Abraham
ran out of the bar and went back home.
For he could not trust the inside.

Abraham stormed back into the house.
Everyone still in the library upstairs.
Abraham saw that Prince Norm was back.

Prince Norm said

"We were waiting for you"?

"Why"? Said, Abraham

"For I have much to show you".

For there was more than just books in the library. Prince Norm blows on a brick wall located behind the bookshelf when he blew on the surface a portal opened to another world. Grassy fields and mountains in the background waterfalls and animals flying in the air.

Abraham was scared to go inside and so was Elizabeth. Prince Norm let them know that it was nothing to be afraid of.

Abraham grabbed Abner's hands and the daughter of Abraham and Elizabeth grabbed Elizabeth's hands.

They walk inside, the portal immediately closes. Abner, Abraham, Elizabeth, and the daughter of Abraham and Elizabeth all felt the difference between earth and this world. The air was smoother, things felt more peaceful, great place to be. (Abraham ducks immediately after he sees a giant dragon flying over his head).

"Abraham shouts there's more like you here"?

"There are many more" said Prince Norm

"Welcome to the Guardian Falls " said Price Norm.

For this is a magical kingdom. In it, you will find and discover many other creatures far from myself. Here in Guardian Falls Prince Norm is much bigger than back on earth.

Everyone hops on Prince Norm's back and he starts flying at the beginning Abraham was afraid because he is terrified of heights. He now realizes how bad of a decision this was to ride on the back of a dragon.

Prince Norm calls Abraham a baby

"Are you really scared? Your such a baby!"

You got wings I don't said Abraham,

Prince Norm begins to laugh. Making the

ride more terrifying for Abraham.

"Okay just wait till I get my feet on this

ground"! said, Abraham

"Calm down" said Elizabeth

"He playing with my emotions" said, Abraham.

"It is quite funny" said Prince Norm.

A few moments later they see a giant tree as tall as a mountain. Its head rose above the clouds.

For it is the tree of wisdom and the tree of high-power. When we arrived the tree with the name of a Gudmor noticed Abner!

"Oh my! is that who I think it is" said Gudmor he begins to laugh ha ha ha ha Ha ha ha

"We are saved at once! For he has risen again". Said Gudmor. "We praise you for your goodness for you have saved us all for this is your kingdom.

Everything here was created to protect and serve you".

"Come here my child"? says Gudmor.

"Touch the root of my branch and there you will receive yet another gift".

Abner did what he was told to do. When he touched the root of the branch that streamed a river of gold. A streak of gold went within his veins for it was not painful, it felt very pleasant. You can see the gold crawling up his bloodstream from his head to his toes.

Abraham got worried and was about to step forward to stop it but Prince Norm put his tail up and blocked him from intruding.

Gudmor ah yes you have received the power of immortality for death will never be upon you but you can cause it.

Appeared on his arm above the feather and above the eye of a tiger showed an ANKH for the ANKH is a symbol of life that holds connotations of immortality when depicted in the hands of the gods.

Abner you have already received three gifts, you must go out and find the rest.

For there are some gifts that are in the hand of evil and must be recaptured.

"He is only 7 what do you expect my son to do"? said, Abraham.

"Do not be blind to what Abner can do for what lies in him will surprise you all. For I am of the same age"

.

"When the day comes you will see and you will fight by Abner's side" says Gudmor.

184

Located near the tree was a heavily guarded village. For you need rest for tomorrow is training day said Gudmor.

"Training day" said Elizabeth

"Yes, training day practice is very important here at Guardian falls you must know how to perform your gifts and the perks that come with each one".

"Follow me" said Prince Norm

Everyone follows Prince Norm to the heavily guarded village. Once at the gate the gatekeepers saw that it was the prince and opened the gate. Inside you had creatures who looked as if they were humans but, really they were Zules. Zules are creatures that appear to be humans but have ears pointed like elves and noses that are pointy. For at night their skin glows when they are at peace. The Zules knew who Abner was and was so amazed when they saw him. They surrounded Abner curious to see if it really was him.

Once they found out word got around quickly that the savior has returned to his kingdom. The Prince continued to escort them to where they will be staying. We went off far pass the crowd and up the hill with many steps. There was a house made out of stone. In front of the house was a mat that said welcomneirs for that is how they say welcome in Guardian Falls.

Inside the home was cozy and comfortable. Everything inside was made out of wood. Get some rest for tomorrow is a big day.

Prince Norm told everyone goodnight and

was on his was.

DAY OF TRAINING

Still in the Guardian Falls away from earth, In the comfortable home that was given to Abner and his family. Knocking on the door was a Zule as beautiful she can be. She was sent to bring Abner and his family to the training arena. For her name was Athena. Athena escorted them to the arena and waiting there was the Prince himself.

I hope you got some rest said the Prince

For today's training will be all in the mind.

Prince Norm opens the giant wooden door.

The entrance into the training arena. He

then walks inside as the rest including

Athena follows. Inside look as if it was an

institution. The rooms look as if it was an

interrogation room and inside were Zules

being mentally trained. In one window I

saw a female Zule that had three medal

balls floating in the air rotating them

around slowly in a triangle shape. Another

room had a male Zule who was controlling the earth like a creature we call a snake.

The next room was empty for it was for me. Standing in the window was Abner's family and inside was the Zule, Abner, and Prince Norm.

Sit there said Prince Norm

There was a metal seat where Abner was told to seat in.

This is just a test to see how strong your brain is Prince Norm said to Abner.

He did not need to connect anything to his body nor his brain because the chair he was sitting in gives them the results and the computer tells them the results within the room as if it was SIRI.

I want you to move this rock I got here said Prince Norm.

He places the rock on the table.

Abner questioned him and said,

But How?

I cannot tell you have to figure it out on your own said Prince Norm.

In front of Abner was a mirror Abner could see the mirror but could not see himself.

He looked at the rock then he closed his eyes. For he did not move the rock he melted it and made it into liquid for no one has ever done that. Prince Norm was amazed.

You turned a stone into liquid how impressive said Prince Norm.

He grabbed another rock and placed it on the metal table same spot as the last one.

This time when Abner closed his eyes a memory from his father's mind attached to his. Abner saw how his father was being beaten by the white riflemen. He saw how his father's soul was ripped straight from out of him. He saw his father left in darkness waiting for him to die. That angered Abner for he did not only move the rock he caused the glass to shatter and the walls to crack. Prince Norm stopped him before he destroyed the building.

You did all of this and this is your first day of training you are truly a GOD said Prince Norm. Abner's family noticed what was going on and were left in shock that their son had powers. Everything that *Gurtle* told them was the complete truth of the book never lies nor the prophecies sent from the GODS. Abner opens his eyes and sees all that he has done. To him, it feels as if something is taking over his body.

Prince Norm said You are becoming stronger for this is a really good sign.

A shofar was blown to warn of danger and danger there was. Prince Norm told them that they were being attacked.

Outside they went. Prince Norm told Abner and his family to stay back because they are not ready.

Ahead was a dragon by the name Havok angry he was by the look in his eye. Zule's ran pass Abner and his family jumping off the ground with great amounts of height. Arrows they had as weapons releasing the bow while in the air. Prince Norm ran while in human form jumping in the air while transforming back into a dragon.

Prince Norm flew above the dragon transforming back into a human child with a mighty sword in his hand piercing the dragon in his neck.

Havok fell to the ground of greater heights. Havok started to spin out of control. Prince Norm tried transforming back into a dragon but....

THE TEMPLE

Dust arose from the ground, spinning in rotation causing a tornado to form. Abner staring directly at it stop it instantly by just looking away. Prince Norm being impressed but, still a little judgemental clapped for Abner. Abner looked at Prince Norm drained he was. His father Abraham watching him from a distance. Abraham is now getting the hang of things even though it took him a while to catch on. He made eye – contact with Avraham for only 2 seconds. Prince Norm stood in his way and told Abner that he wanted to take him to the Guardian temple.

The Guardian temple is a sacred place where only the chosen ones remained. Those who ruled here once before will always be remembered. For their memory remains inside the tomb guarded within Guardian falls temple. Abner went alone, Abraham did not know of his leavings. In the air they are. Abner's hair blows through the wind watching the birds fly past him. These are the typical average birds we see on earth. For these birds were ancient Archaeopteryx. Usually, you don't see birds and dragons flying in the same area but, since Prince Norm is half human it really does not matter in this case.

Ahead of the clouds disappear as they reach their destination. On the building grew moss, long were the stairs, huge statues of the king who once ruled stood tall. For it was the first thing you can see. A big body of water surrounded it, So the only way to this temple was by flight or by boat. Stood amongst the gate were

Grimers – Grimers protect the gates of Guardian falls. Grimers are heavy built creatures with giant ears and a big nose. Their bodies are made out of stone. They were made to easily blend in to capture suspicious activity or danger near or by Guardian falls temple. For they have a large reputation here at Guardian falls but, evil Zules tend not to pay them any attention. Everything in the world of guardian falls is not of good, for there is much evil that creeps on the surface of this magical world.

Inside Prince Norm and Abner are now in. Three ways we have to choose from one lead to the right destination the other two no one knows or hopes to find out. They choose to go left. Prince Norm knows the way, this not his first time being in the Guardian Falls temple. Abner and Prince

Norm are in for an experience. Dark it was inside encrypted on the wall were symbols from the GODS. They did not become noticeable until Prince Norm (Dragon Form) blew down the hallway and came lit were the torches. The hall was very long it looked as if it was a dead end. The temple was not that easy when they came across it. Booby – traps were there surrounding them but, they were not triggered. Good for Abner and Prince Norm.

Far along they went and there lied a body of sparkling water. It appeared as if it wasn't even real. Along the walls were sparkling crystals and gems. Out appeared a golden object, the face of a woman popping through the wall. Hard and solid it felt and cold it was. You can tell that around the neck area was an object that appeared to be a necklace. The necklace was missing. Abner turned around and in the rich body of water laying on the surface of the ground was a shiny object flashing in the eyes of Abner. Prince Norm

(Human Form) picked it up! In his hand was the necklace. He places the object back around the neck of the golden face. A strong vibration, we felt in the temple. Cracked in half was the face and split open went the wall. It opened as a doorway. Abner and Prince Norm watched the secret gateway open. For Prince Norm has never discovered this before.

When the wall completely opened appeared was a mist of dust and once the dust was cleared appeared a tomb. Surrounding the tomb were serpents of two. When they saw Abner and Prince Norm (Human Form) they transformed into Blood Zules- A Blood Zule evil or good. There eyes bloodshot red, veins are in sight of there skin. Gorgeous they can be but, it's the curse of an illusion. Laying next the tomb were these creatures that looked as if they were human but, up close you can tell that It is a Blood Zule.

The question is why? Before Prince Norm gets a word out. The Blood Zule to the right of Prince Norm questioned them saying,

"Why have you interrupt the queen" In a voice that has a great amount of bass.

Prince Norm and Abner had no idea what the Blood Zule was talking about. For they remained silent.

The blood Zule questions them yet again.

"Are you of Death?" Why have you interrupt the queen?

"What queen"? asked Abner.

Opened flew the tom. A skeleton hand arose from it. Out comes the full body skeleton with a crown of a queen on its head. The minute her feet hit the ground, her skeleton toes no longer visible became skin. Appeared in front of Abner and Price Norm was a woman. A formal queen she was from millions of years ago. Long nails and beautiful hair she had. She clothed herself in the bodies of the Blood Zules. Prince Norm and Abner afraid for they have met and awaken a formal God/Queen by the name of CEZEL. She gazes at Abner, for she knows who he is. Cezel laughs and says.

(Laughing out loud) "So, you found yourself a new body"!

Abner was confused, He has no memory of what he once was. Cezel rubs the skin of his Abner's face.

"So Young," said, Cezel

Risen from the tomb was the mother of Abner. Heavily skilled in magic and strength. Prince Norm introduces himself. Cezel stops him and says.

"I know who you are"!

Prince Norm responded. "You do"?

Your father was a good man.

"How do you know my father," said Prince

Norm

TO BE CONTINUED

Next book unfolds what happened to Prince Norm while attacking the dragon and how does the queen know about his father.

Don't forget to leave a Review

You will never forget Black Child for Abner will always be with you.

Lightning Source UK Ltd.
Milton Keynes UK
UKHW022134200223
417354UK00006B/172